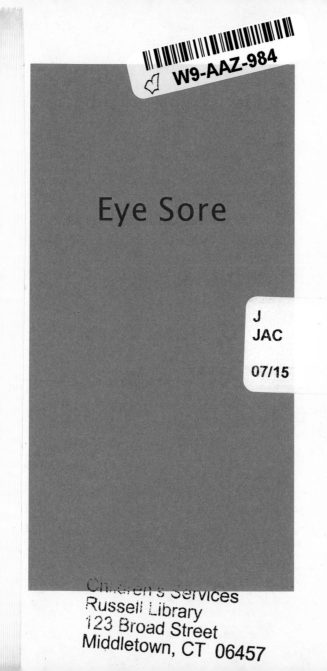

Eye Sore

Eye Sore

Melanie Jackson

Orca currents

ORCA BOOK PUBLISHERS

Library and Archives Canada Cataloguing in Publication

Jackson, Melanie, 1956-, author
Eye sore / Melanie Jackson.
(Orca currents)

Issued in print and electronic formats.
ISBN 978-1-4598-0771-6 (pbk.). — ISBN 978-1-4598-0773-0 (pdf). —
ISBN 978-1-4598-0774-7 (epub)

I. Title. II. Series: Orca currents
PS8569.A265E94 2015   jc813'.6   c2014-906667-8
c2014-906668-6

First published in the United States, 2015
Library of Congress Control Number: 2014952057

Summary: Chaz has to solve a mystery that threatens his father's new business
venture of operating a Ferris wheel similar to the London Eye.

*Orca Book Publishers is dedicated to preserving the environment and has
printed this book on Forest Stewardship Council® certified paper.*

Orca Book Publishers gratefully acknowledges the support for its
publishing programs provided by the following agencies: the Government
of Canada through the Canada Book Fund and the Canada Council for the Arts,
and the Province of British Columbia through the BC Arts Council
and the Book Publishing Tax Credit.

Cover photography by Shutterstock
Author photo by Bart Jackson

ORCA BOOK PUBLISHERS
PO Box 5626, Stn. B
Victoria, BC Canada
V8R 6S4

ORCA BOOK PUBLISHERS
PO Box 468
Custer, WA USA
98240-0468

www.orcabook.com
Printed and bound in Canada.

18 17 16 15 • 4 3 2 1

To Bart, SNJ and Lynne

Chapter One

Liftoff. The Eye glided backward and up, and I watched the earth drain away. I broke into a sweat. I clutched the edge of my seat.

Beside me, Dad exclaimed, "The Eye is going to put North Vancouver on the map, Chaz. It's going to put *us* on the map."

He clapped me on the back. Bad idea. My breakfast was hovering around chest level, ready for its own liftoff.

We swung up into the fir trees. They surrounded us like curtains. I took a deep breath. It wasn't so bad when I didn't look down.

I needed to get through the twenty-minute ride without being sick or passing out. I didn't want to spoil this important day for Dad.

Today was the official opening of the Eye, near the base of Grouse Mountain. Dad had poured all of his money into it. He'd borrowed a ton more. Giving North Vancouver its own Eye had been his dream ever since he'd visited the London Eye a few years back.

I just wished Dad's dream didn't involve heights.

Don't get me wrong. I understood the appeal. With their steel spokes and glass gondolas, Eyes shone like stars.

The city of Nanchang, in China, even called its Eye the Star. There was also the Texas Star in Dallas.

Dad's Eye was smaller than those in London and other places. He'd modeled it on the first Ferris wheel, as Eyes used to be called. An engineer, George Ferris Jr., built the original wheel for the 1893 Chicago World's Fair. George had been trying to outdo the big hit of the world's fair in Paris, the Eiffel Tower.

Like George's wheel, Dad's was 264 feet high. It had thirty-six gondolas, each the size of a minivan.

Some Eye owners crammed people in. Not Dad. He wanted his riders to appreciate the beauty of the scenery— not be crushed by other bodies giving off BO. He designed each gondola for only ten people, with cushioned seats around the glass sides.

Dad would hold the first official ride in an hour, for local VIPs. The press would be on board, too, snapping photos and filming.

Dad was giving me this private ride as a special treat.

I couldn't let on how sick I felt. I couldn't let him know I suffered from vertigo. I'd hidden it all these years.

I couldn't let Dad down today of all days.

Our gondola swung higher. The fir trees thinned out. The wide hills popular with skiers in winter stretched below.

I felt my breakfast waving along with them.

I turned away from Dad. I shut my eyes.

"A dream come true for a boy, huh, Chaz?" Dad asked.

I caught the anxious note in Dad's voice. He knew I didn't want to work for him this summer. He knew I wasn't thrilled about selling Eye tickets day after day.

What I wanted to do this summer was go to dance camp. I wanted to shuffle my feet. I had already tap-danced through several musicals at school and the community center. I was getting into break dancing too. Forget spinning on an Eye. I could spin on the palm of my hand.

In a few weeks our community center was holding a talent contest. You could dance, sing, tell jokes or do whatever your talent was. The prize was a trip to New York City. A tour of the Big Apple. And the winner would get to perform for a talent agent.

Dance camp would have meant whole days of practice. I could have polished my routines and had all sorts of coaching to help me prepare for the talent contest.

Of course, I'd practice even without the upcoming contest. To me, dance was everything.

It's great to have a dream, Son, but if you're going to have any chance of making a dream come true, you need capital. It took me years to save up for the Eye, but I did it. You need to learn how to buckle down and work for your dreams.

Dad wanted me to be practical.

To be like him.

That's why I couldn't let him know I had vertigo. He needed me. I couldn't fail him.

So, for the whole summer, I was stuck here.

We rose to the top of the Eye. Sun filled the gondola. It was too bright to see anything—as long as I didn't look down.

Dad was trying out a new phone app called *Don't Look Now, But...* He'd been excited to download the app, which tracked height above sea level. "Wow, look at these numbers climb!"

I couldn't. I shut my eyes.

"Wait. They're leveling. They're dropping! Whoa. Time for the big plunge!"

The gondola churned down through pure blue sky. The skyscrapers of Vancouver jutted into view. Then, dipping farther, the gondola seemed like it was going to dive into Burrard Inlet.

Dad nudged me. He held up his phone. The sea-level numbers spun down. To me it was a countdown to a major barf.

I clapped a hand over my eyes. This was it. I was going to heave. "I can't believe this," I muttered.

Dad laughed, misreading my reaction. "I can hardly believe it either. Pretty cool app, huh?"

He clicked the phone off. "Hey, look at all the people below. I'd hoped for a good crowd, but…"

His voice trailed off.

Curious, I peeked out from under my hand.

The chain-link fence surrounding the Eye stretched below us. Behind the fence was a crowd, all right.

But you couldn't describe it as a good crowd.

People pumped fists. They waved signs. *Eye Wrecks Our View. Eye Spy A Monster. Close the Eye.*

Pale, bewildered, Dad turned to me. "I don't understand. City hall gave us the go-ahead. We had the permits. We gave the press a tour of the construction site. We got publicity. All that time, no one protested."

I shook my head. I didn't get it either. I wanted to say something to make him feel better. But first I had to get rid of my dizziness.

The mob spotted Dad in the gondola. They pointed and shouted. They pushed against the fence. The fence bent under their weight. They were going to smash it down.

Chapter Two

The woods swooped up to greet us as we headed toward the landing platform.

My buddy Moe Jenkins opened the gondola doors. Moe was also working the Eye this summer. Our duties were to take tickets, help people on and off the gondolas and keep the place tidy.

Moe knew my secret. He knew about the vertigo. He wouldn't blab though.

In fact, Moe didn't say much of anything to anyone. He was a guy of few words.

Dad and I stepped off. I sat down on the edge of the platform. Earth. Solid, reassuring earth. I was shaky with relief.

I didn't relax for long. The protesters were hurling insults at Dad. "Close it down, Higgins!"

Higgins was Don Higgins, my dad.

"Take your idiotic Eye somewhere else, will ya? We don't want it!"

Others picked up that last part. "*We don't want it!*"

"What's going on?" Dad demanded, looking at Moe.

Moe was as pale as Dad. He pulled a newspaper from his back pocket. He handed it to Dad.

The paper was the *North Vancouver Express*. Under a photo of the Eye, a huge headline blared:

Eye will make your property worthless!

Dad scanned the article. In disgust, he threw it to the ground. "I gotta stop those people before they trample us."

He ran over to the mob. Moe and I started to follow him. He gestured for us to stay.

I could guess Dad's thoughts. He was worried the mob might turn violent.

By now they'd pushed the fence so far that it was bending in a diagonal.

A long sandbox stretched beside the fence. The box, for our toddler patrons, gleamed with fresh white sand and brand-new red pails and shovels.

Dad stepped into the sandbox. He was standing right under the fence. "Please, everybody! Let's talk about what's bothering you!"

Some of the protesters stopped yelling. Others kept on. But they stopped shoving at the fence. Maybe they saw that if they continued, they'd plow Dad under.

Or maybe they'd noticed the TV crew that had just pulled up to one side. They didn't want to be caught on film destroying property.

I picked up the newspaper. The story was by Jonas Bilk, owner of the *North Vancouver Express*.

I didn't know Jonas. But I knew his son. Brody Bilk was in my year at school. Brody was a husky blond football player. Being in theater arts, I didn't have a lot to do with Brody. He had a goofy, likable grin. From a distance he seemed like a decent guy.

I skimmed his dad's article. *This oversized wheel is ugly…cheap tourist attraction…strangers barging through our quiet neighborhood…*

Jonas finished off his article with *Thinking of selling your home for a good price? Of moving, or retiring? Forget it! Don Higgins just wrecked that dream for you.*

It was so unfair. My dad was a dream builder, not a dream wrecker. Like his idol, George Ferris, he'd risked everything to build the Eye.

I thought of something. At first people had said George Ferris's wheel was ugly. They'd said no one would want to ride it.

Once things quieted down, I would remind Dad of that. It might make him feel better.

Dad was talking to the protesters, and they were listening. Dad had that going for him—he was a master salesperson.

"I'd be glad to meet with you about the Eye. I *want* to hear your concerns," he was saying as the TV cameras whirred.

"We want your wheel outta here!" somebody shouted.

It was a hoarse voice. A voice that had been doing a lot of shouting.

"Ssshhhh!" people said. They were looking embarrassed. They'd come here because of Jonas Bilk's article. Now they could see Dad was a regular guy, not a monster.

Except for that one person at the back. He let out a couple more yells.

Dad held up his hands. "Let me look into getting a meeting room. A school gym, maybe, or a hall. We'll talk, okay?"

People nodded. Some of them walked away. Others formed groups of three or four and talked in low tones.

Dad's phone rang. He saw the name on the display, and his face lit up. "Mr. Mayor!" he exclaimed.

Then he looked worried again. "I understand, sir," he said.

He turned his back to the TV crew. Quietly he told Moe and me, "The mayor's canceled. So have all the other guests. After Jonas Bilk's article, no one wants to be seen here."

"Bummer," Moe said. For Moe, that was talkative.

I looked past the remaining protesters. The road to the Eye wound down through thick trees and out of sight. "Jonas has it wrong," I objected. "The Eye's not in a neighborhood."

Dad shook his head. "Everything is optics, son. It's what you can make people see. It doesn't matter if it's real or not. Jonas wants to sell papers. What better way than to get people angry? He's just doing what I'm doing. He's being a businessman."

Dad walked over to the small office beside the Eye. It wasn't his usual bouncy, go-get-'em walk. His head was down. His shoulders were slumped.

I thought of running after him. Of reminding him about the challenges George Ferris had overcome.

But I had a feeling that Dad wanted to be alone.

I glanced at the ticket booth. Moe and I were supposed to be starting our jobs about now. We should be selling tickets to the hordes of visitors Dad expected.

Not one person was lined up.

However, someone was at the fence. Fingers clutching the chain links, he was swinging the fence back and forth.

And jeering at me.

"Hey, dancing boy," Brody Bilk called. "What you gonna do? *Now that my dad's destroyed your dad.*"

Chapter Three

Brody's voice was hoarse. It was Brody I'd heard yelling after everyone else quieted down.

So much for the good-natured guy with the goofy grin.

I called back, "Maybe you could leave the fence alone? It's about to fall over."

That was the wrong thing to say. Brody wrenched harder at it. "*Make* me leave it alone, dancing boy."

The people beyond the fence, who'd been talking in groups, turned to watch us. My face burned.

Brody climbed on the fence. He stuck his feet through the chain links. He called, "Dance for me, loser. Then maybe I'll leave your stupid fence alone."

He swung hard on the fence. It gave out long, agonized creaks. One of the posts came out of the ground.

The TV crew had been heading down the road to their van. Hearing Brody's taunts, they stopped. Raising their cameras, they ran back toward the Eye.

I couldn't let Brody demolish the fence. But it was either that or total humiliation.

It looked like I'd have to dance.

I launched into a soft-shoe routine. Soft shoe is a tap dance without metal plates attached to your shoes. I hopped on my left foot. Then I brushed sideways with my right sole.

As I danced, I got an idea. Dancing always helped me think. It woke up the brain cells, got 'em moving.

I kept hop-stepping with my left foot and brushing sideways with my right. I was heading toward Brody, who was rocking on the fence and smirking.

I started leaning harder to my right. Picking up speed.

The TV crew reached Brody. They aimed their cameras at us. There is nothing the folks at home enjoy more than watching someone getting humiliated.

Brody flashed a grin at the cameras. He turned back to me. "Think of it this way. You're my monkey on a chain."

I was closing in on the sandbox. I didn't want to run into the box's edge. I had something else planned.

With my right foot, I brushed sideways one last time. I retreated several steps. Then I ran forward, still sideways, and leaped.

I kept my feet together. I was sailing down in a feet-first diagonal. I had my arms raised to offset some of my weight, like a parachute.

I landed on the sides of my runners. My soles sprayed up a huge cloud of sand—right into Brody's face.

The sand got into his mouth and eyes. Choking, he fell back from the fence.

The TV crew focused in on him.

Like I said, I had to make a choice between letting the fence get wrecked and total humiliation.

Brody's humiliation.

Sorry. I guess I left that part out.

Dad marched toward me. I grinned at him. I'd showed up Brody Bilk.

My grin lasted all of three seconds. Dad's face was stony. He brushed past me, hissing, "You idiot! That's all I need now—Jonas Bilk's kid injured!"

Dad swept out the gate. He barked at the TV crew to turn their cameras off. He helped Brody up. "I'm sorry. My son got carried away. Can I get you a cold drink? A towel?"

I wasn't in the mood to eat lunch in the office. Not with Dad there, radiating grimness. Instead, I took my lunch into the woods behind the office. It was quiet and shady, with dark ferns and pale wildflowers.

I liked the woods. By law, nothing could disturb them. They were part of a protected ecosystem. In buying the land,

Dad had agreed not to dig up, develop or otherwise disrupt this part of the property.

I slumped down against a tree trunk. I ate my sandwich. It was my favorite, Swiss cheese, onions, mayo, loads of black pepper. I'd made it myself. I barely tasted it. I was too bummed out. All Dad cared about was his stupid Eye.

Okay. The Eye wasn't *all* he cared about. But it sure felt that way.

I cracked the top off a Gatorade bottle and gulped the drink down. I let out a loud belch.

Above me, there was a fluttering sound. I glimpsed a streak of red.

"You frightened a goldfinch away," said a voice behind me.

It was a short man with gray hair. He was on the other side of the chain-link fence. His eyes twinkled at me behind round gold-rimmed glasses. He was holding a zoom-lens camera.

"Bird-watching," the man explained. He had a brisk, cheerful accent. German, maybe.

"I saw you scowling. You are having a—how do you say—lousy day?" With his camera he gestured to the sky. "Watch the birds! How they fly about. So graceful. It will make you happy again."

"Uh…okay."

"Look up, up!"

Smiling, the man trotted off.

I stood up. I even looked up, like he told me to do. He sure made bird-watching sound appealing. Watch the birds, forget your troubles.

The only thing was, it hadn't been a goldfinch that I'd scared. That flash of red was a robin.

If you were into bird-watching, wouldn't you know that?

Chapter Four

I rang the Bilks' doorbell a third time.
With any luck, they weren't home.

I was here to apologize to Brody.
I'd walked from the Eye.

The apology was Dad's idea.
I thought Dad was wrong. Brody had
acted like a bully.

But, with the troubles Dad was
having, I didn't argue. I'd heard him

on the phone with his bank manager. Two tour groups had canceled. Nobody wanted to be near a shouting mob.

Unless people started showing up, Dad would have to close the Eye.

No one was answering the Bilks' door. I used the time to get some moves in.

Hop, slide, spin. *Jump!*

In midair, I folded my knees. I wrapped my arms around them. I'd seen the late, great dancer Gene Kelly do this in an old movie. I was thinking of including it in my talent-show routine.

I let go of my knees—too late. Unlike Gene, I didn't land neatly on two feet. I landed on my right foot and fell sideways. My right hand plunged deep into the soil of a planter.

"Are you looking for something in there?"

The door was open. A girl was staring down at me.

"Uh..." I pulled my hand free. It was caked with dirt. I stood up. "I'm looking for Brody Bilk."

She glanced at the planter. "You won't find him in there."

"No," I agreed. I was trying not to stare at the girl. She was about my age. She had the Bilk blond hair and blue eyes.

Brody's sister? I didn't know he had one.

She sure was pretty. It was truly amazing how the same family features rearranged could be so much nicer to look at. Like, for hours.

I cleared my throat. "I don't think I've seen you around. I mean, I would have noticed."

Smooth, Higgins.

She didn't reply. There was a glimmer in her blue eyes though. It may have been amusement.

I tried a different tack. "My name is Chaz Higgins. I'm—"

"I know who you are. You're the boy who humiliated my cousin on TV."

She shut the door.

But didn't slam it, I thought.

I jumped down from the step and executed a soft-shoe hop, slide and circle. *She didn't slam it*.

But I still had to apologize. I couldn't leave without doing that. Otherwise I would be letting Dad down yet again.

It was a warm night. Maybe Brody was in the backyard.

I walked around the side of the house. A gardener was clipping a hedge. I thought he might notice me and say something. But he didn't. He had his earbuds in. I could hear the tinny buzz of his music.

A terrace stretched behind the house. Jonas Bilk was sitting on a patio chair. He was slurping back lemonade from a tall glass.

"Excuse me, sir," I said.

Jonas didn't answer. I saw that he was wearing earbuds too.

I stepped up to the terrace. The glass doors stood open. I looked through to a round foyer with a white marble floor. A white marble staircase curved against a white wall.

Okay, so now I had a pretty good idea of the Bilks' color scheme.

But not about where Brody was.

Brody's cousin walked across the foyer. She was holding a magazine.

She, too, was wearing earbuds.

Now I got why it had taken three doorbell rings for someone to answer the door. Everybody was listening to tunes.

I waved my arms to get her attention.

She glanced over at me, startled.

On the wall beside her was a portrait of a woman in a white dress. The woman, holding a glowing white flower, was blond and pretty.

She looked a lot like Brody's cousin. An ancestor?

From upstairs, a bloodcurdling scream burst out. Followed by a woman's voice saying "Enough! *Please stop!*"

I ran up to Brody's cousin. "We have to get upstairs."

She removed her earbuds. "What are you talking about?"

"I just heard a weird scream. Like someone being tortured. Then a woman calling for help."

I started up the twisting staircase.

She caught my arm. "*What* call for help?"

"Lauren, what's going on?"

Brody appeared at the top of the stairs. Seeing me, he jumped down them two at a time. "You! Get out!"

"Somebody screamed."

"It was the TV. Mom's watching a horror movie."

It was a sensible explanation. I hesitated.

Brody demanded, "What are you doing here anyway?"

I decided to get the apology over with. "Sorry about the sand thing." I held out my hand.

He stared at it. His face turned an angry, boiling red.

Oh, right. My hand was still covered with soil. With my left hand, I brushed the soil off. I brought my right hand forward for apology, take two.

"Get out of here, Higgins," Brody barked.

"But..." I didn't want to get out. I wanted to get to know Lauren Bilk.

I couldn't say this. So I did what I always do when stuck for words. I executed a dance step. I did a long sideways slide.

Brody looked ready to pop. What

was it about dancing—*my* dancing—
that burned the guy up?

For a finale, I raised my arms.

"*Out!*" Brody bellowed.

Okay, so I hadn't won Brody over
with my soft-shoe routine.

But as I turned to leave, I caught
Lauren smiling.

The next morning, Dad, Moe and I
headed up to open the Eye. Dad slapped
the steering wheel. He was cheerful
again. "We have another chance!"

A TV crew was coming. They weren't
going to film protesters this time. They
were going to ride the Eye. Dad had
convinced them it would be fun for their
viewers.

It would also bring us great publicity.
It would make up for yesterday.

Dad opened the gate with his remote.
He swung the car up behind the office.

"Okay, guys. The TV people will be here at ten. We have two hours to polish the Eye till it shines."

We got out of the car. On the other side of the office, the Eye rose like a gigantic silver coin. Shine it? It was already gleaming so brightly we had to shield our eyes with our hands.

"Not much for us to do," I said.

There was a clanking sound at Moe's feet. We looked down.

He'd accidentally kicked an empty paint can. The inside of the can was coated with black. It gaped up at us like a bruise.

Ahead, we spotted more empty cans. We glanced at each other.

We hurried around the office to the Eye.

More paint cans littered the ground.

We looked up.

The bottom third of the Eye was drenched in black.

Chapter Five

Overnight, someone had vandalized the big wheel.

Moe, Dad and I stared. The gondolas and spokes at the middle still sparkled. At its base, though, the Eye was—well, a black Eye.

"Brody Bilk," I said. I pictured him tossing paint cans over the fence.

Then climbing the fence and hurling their contents at the Eye.

Dad looked at me sharply. "You don't know it was Brody. You can't accuse someone because you don't like him."

He took his car keys out. "I'll go get paint remover. Moe, you come with me. Chaz, you stay here and clean up what you can."

I picked up the paint cans. I carried them to the Dumpster at the back. I threw them in as hard as I could. I took grim pleasure in hearing them smash against the metal sides.

I remembered the hatred in Brody's face. I could hear him sneering, *Hey, dancing boy...*

Dad was wrong. I did know, without a doubt. Brody was the vandal.

I looked up at the Eye. To Dad, it was a dream come true. To the Bilks, it was an evil Eye.

To me, it was a source of my arch-enemy, vertigo.

The three of us tackled the black paint. We started with the gondola beside the platform. We scrubbed its sides. We climbed on top to scrub the gondola's roof.

Moe glanced at me. I guessed what he was thinking. Didn't I feel dizzy?

I gave him a thumbs-up. The gondola was only ten feet high. Places I could jump down from didn't bother me. It was the higher ones that got to me, big spaces with too much air—too much space—between me and the ground.

We didn't speak as we worked. The only sounds were from the forest around us until—

Can you believe, baby, how good it feels
Falling in love on a Ferris wheel?

It was Dad's phone, with its Michael Sarver ringtone. He patted down his pockets to find it. He was always forgetting where he'd put it. Then he spotted the phone on top of a picnic table.

I looked way up to the top of the Eye, to the blue sky beyond.

All at once I was tired of being scared of heights. I was tired of having to hide it from Dad. If vertigo was a person, not a feeling, I would punch its daylights out.

We finished cleaning that first gondola. In the control booth, Dad rotated the Eye. The next gondola shifted down to the base. We started on that.

We were still working when the TV crew arrived.

"You're the dancing guy."

The reporter beamed at me. She held the microphone up to my face.

Her cameraman aimed his lens at us.

"Chaz isn't here to dance," Dad said.

By now Dad had rotated the Eye so that the black parts were at the top. He gestured to them. He smiled at the reporter. "As you can see, we're still working on the look of the Eye."

The reporter barely glanced at the Eye. Her gaze was fixed on me. "I was hoping your son would dance for us, like he did yesterday. Maybe he could do a two-step."

A two-step? That would be boring. A two-step just means moving one foot sideways, forward or back, then sliding your other foot to meet it.

"I could do much better than that," I assured her. As well as the Gene Kelly midair move, I was working on a spin. A fast one, like skaters do. Followed by a leap in the air, then a rapid hop-slide-jump.

Dad's hand tightened around my shoulders. He said brightly, "Chaz is going to do *way* better than that. He's going to take you and your cameraman up in the Eye."

Dad turned his smile on me. He was showing he believed in me. "Chaz will give you a guided tour. Then you can share it on tonight's news for your thousands of viewers. Right, son?"

"I…uh…Let me check this out with Moe," I said.

"*What?*" Dad exclaimed.

But I was striding away from him and the TV people. I joined Moe at the ticket booth. Moe was reading *Scalpel Monthly*. He read medical stuff all the time. He wanted to become a surgeon, like his dad.

"You gotta help me," I said in a low voice.

Moe looked up from his magazine.

"I'm stuck going up in the Eye with those TV people," I said. "Tell me what to do about my vertigo."

"Duh. Tell your Dad about it," he answered.

I glanced back. Dad and the TV crew were staring at me. Dad was frowning. The reporter wore a puzzled smile. The cameraman was filming me.

I waved cheerily at them. "That's not an option."

"Oh, man." Moe exhaled heavily. He thought for a moment. "Okay. Stand still. Shut your eyes. If you look at something—a tree, the water, the city—it won't be moving. But your body is moving. That's what confuses your brain. That's what makes you dizzy."

I stared at him. "That's amazing."

I didn't mean *what* Moe had said. I meant *how much* he'd said. Normally Moe didn't say that many words in an entire year.

Chapter Six

The reporter was going to be on camera, so she took off her sunglasses. She started to place them in her purse.

"Wait," I said. *Shades!* That's what I needed. With shades on, I could close my eyes and no one would know.

"Do you mind if I borrow those?" I asked.

She looked at me doubtfully. The sunglasses were neon pink with rhinestones.

"It's fine," I assured her. "I forgot my own. The sun gives me a headache."

We stepped into the Eye. I put the sunglasses on. So what if I appeared on TV wearing them? It had to be better than barfing in front of thousands of viewers.

The cameraman started filming. I closed my eyes.

The reporter said brightly, "We're on the new North Vancouver Eye, built by Don Higgins. With us for the ride is Don's son, Chaz. Up, up, we go. Wheee! I can feel my stomach churning. How about you, Chaz?"

I smiled and shrugged. I didn't want to speak. My breakfast was stirring in my stomach, as if searching for an exit. I thought it was better to keep the floodgates closed, just in case.

As the Eye climbed higher, I realized Moe was right. The movement was bearable if I didn't look at anything. It wasn't great, but it wasn't bad.

The reporter hastily filled the silence. "Here we go, out of the trees, into the wild blue yonder! So, Chaz. Why do Ferris wheels go counterclockwise? I've always wondered. I bet our viewers at home are curious too."

I realized I couldn't stay silent. Not while trapped in a gondola with Ms. Buzzing-With-Questions.

Keeping my eyes shut, I replied, "In the old days, people were afraid of a forward-spinning wheel. They thought it would push the motor off the wheel's base. The wheel would then spin off and roll away."

The reporter let out a whistle. "Imagine this Eye rolling down the highway and *splash!* Into Burrard Inlet!"

I didn't like the Eye. It took me away from dancing. But some outsider finding fault with the Eye—that was different. The Eye was my dad's dream.

I tried to keep the annoyance out of my voice. "Our Eye isn't going to roll anywhere, ma'am. As far as we know, no Ferris wheel has ever rolled off its base. Even when a hurricane hit Chicago in 1893, George Ferris's wheel stayed put. A runaway wheel is just one of those myths."

She started to speak, but I cut her off. I was on my own roll.

"Eyes go backward to make the ride more exciting. Think about it. You lift slowly back and up. You reach the sky. The sun blitzes down on you. Then the wheel plunges forward. It hurls you down at the city, the water, the trees below. The whole ride builds up to that big finale."

I stopped. To my surprise, I was actually enthusiastic.

The reporter nodded. She looked pleased.

Wait.

I could see how she looked.

While I'd been talking, I'd opened my eyes.

I was doing exactly what Moe said not to.

I clamped my eyelids shut again. But it was too late. My breakfast churned. I was going to be sick. On TV.

I pointed ahead. "Aim the camera there!" I croaked.

Startled, the cameraman swung his camera. It was a good view of the gleaming beaches of West Vancouver, the blue ocean, the bright horizon.

I sank to the gondola's floor. I pressed my face against my knees. I clenched my teeth. I sweated in the sun. I willed the sick feeling to stay that—just a feeling.

The reporter joked, "We can just about see Hawaii, huh, Chaz?…Er, Chaz?"

The sun slipped off me. The Eye had dropped into the trees again. The gondola cooled down.

I could handle this. I could.

Forcing a smile, I pointed through the gondola's glass floor. "This is how *I* like to ride the Eye."

The reporter plunked down beside me. "Oooh! I see what you mean." She beckoned to the cameraman. "Look at the earth rushing up to us! Look at those trees surging into view! Wow!"

I shut my eyes. *Surging* wasn't a great word to use around me right now.

I was locking up the visitors' gate at the end of the day. We'd had a few riders, but not many.

Moe had already left. I was staying behind, waiting for our new overnight security guard. If our vandal showed up again, the guard would be ready for him.

Dad was on his way to a meeting with the protesters over at the community center. He was hoping to straighten things out.

He brushed grimly past me. I wasn't surprised. Earlier, when I'd stepped off the gondola, I'd forgotten to take off the neon-pink sunglasses. I'd been too busy feeling relieved about not barfing.

I'd seen the look Dad shot me. It was bewildered, exasperated. He thought I had been joking around with the glasses. Not taking business seriously.

No matter how hard I tried, I kept disappointing Dad.

I watched him drive out the back way. Dust from the dirt road rose behind him like a clenched fist. Which pretty much summed up our relationship.

I leaned my forehead against the gate. I thought of the fist-like cloud of dust. I thought of the vertigo.

I punched one of my own fists in the air. *Take that, vertigo!* Then the other fist. I kept doing it. I kept shadowboxing in the shade of the giant Eye.

Pow! Pow-ditty-pow-pow! I was hearing music in my head. I was punching to a beat.

I slid-hopped-jumped in a circle. I imagined fists popping out of the ground. I punched back as I danced. *Pow! Pow!*

Maybe this could be my routine for the talent show. An *angry* dance. Yeah. Why not?

I also imagined audience applause. I pictured Lauren Bilk, clapping louder than anyone.

Wait. I slid to a stop. That was real clapping I heard.

Not by Lauren Bilk though.

It was her cousin, Brody. My enemy.

But he didn't look like an enemy now. He was smiling.

"Hey, buddy! Time we had a talk. Smoothed things over."

Chapter Seven

A *Keeping You Safe Security* van pulled up behind Brody. A security guard got out.

I let him in the gate. I let Brody in too. I didn't see what damage he could do. He was wearing a knapsack, but it was pretty flat. As in, no paint-can shapes bulging out. Besides, I doubted he'd want to mess with the *Keeping You*

Safe guy. The guard was even bigger than Brody, and he was beefy and mean-looking.

I had another reason for letting Brody in. Dad wanted me to get along with him. Maybe Brody really did want to smooth things over.

I still thought he was the one who'd thrown paint over the Eye. But, like Dad said, I had no proof.

I tried to make my voice friendly. I told Brody, "Yeah, we should talk. But first I have to show the guard around."

He beamed. "Sure. I'll wait."

His pleasure seemed real. Had I misjudged the guy?

Brody wandered off.

I took the guard into the office. On the desk, Dad had left a printout with info for him. As the guard read, I kept glancing out the window. The suspicious part of me—in other words, 98 percent—thought Brody might use the opportunity to vandalize the Eye again. Hurl rocks at the gondola windows, say.

But Brody wasn't around the Eye.

Maybe he'd got tired of waiting and left. I went outside. I called his name.

"Over here, buddy!"

I found him in the woods. He was holding his phone.

"Love nature," he explained. He leaned back, aimed his phone high and snapped.

He'd caught a shot of fir branches against blue sky. Didn't seem that exciting a shot to me. The branches would come out dark.

This was the second time I'd found someone taking photos in these woods. First the gray-haired man outside the fence, now Brody inside. I wondered what was so appealing about the place. Especially since the man and Brody had aimed their cameras upward. You could do that anywhere.

Brody stuck his hand out. "Sorry about yesterday. About insulting you. The dancing, I mean. I think it's great that your dad lets you…"

He paused and reddened. "I got carried away. You know, the crowd, the excitement."

I didn't know, no. But he could be telling the truth.

"Okay," I said. I wasn't sure I meant it. I shook his hand anyway. It was what Dad wanted.

Brody kept standing there with that goofy grin I knew from school. I wasn't sure what he expected. Maybe, now that we were buddies, I was supposed to offer him a free spin on the Eye. Or shoot a few baskets with him.

"Uh…I have plans for tonight," I said. And I did. I was going to head over to the community center. Practice some steps in the studio.

"Yeah, I got plans too. A lesson across town," said Brody. He stuffed his phone into a pocket. "Basketball," he added quickly. "As opposed to sewing, say." He forced a laugh.

I stared at him. Brody being friendly was weirder than Brody being a bully.

I walked him to the gate. In his knapsack, something clanked like spoons.

He said, "So drop by sometime, huh?"

Dad came back to the Eye after his meeting. He wore a wide, happy grin.

"The meeting went great—thanks to you! Sure, a few people brought protest signs. But most said how entertaining you were on the news. First, dance-kicking sand into young Brody's face. Second, your on-the-floor routine on the gondola."

Startled, pleased, I took a deep breath. "That wasn't a routine, Dad. I have—"

"Now everyone wants to ride the Eye with their noses pressed to the floor." Dad laughed and shook his head. "I owe you an apology, son. I've been closed-minded. You are one creative performer. And funny! From now on, I'm going to encourage you.

"And hey, as our profits build, we should think about commercials— starring you, high up on the Eye. Real *Eye-catchers*," he joked.

"They'd be that," I said.

Dad was too excited to notice the uneasy note in my voice. "Jonas Bilk showed up. I invited him to speak, but he just thanked me for holding the meeting. I guess he saw how things were and gave up trying to make trouble."

I told Dad about Brody coming by and about us smoothing things over, at Brody's suggestion.

He nodded, pleased. "That can't have been easy for you, son. I know how you feel about Brody."

Dad said he'd meet me at home after my studio practice. We'd order Chinese.

I jogged down the hill toward the community center. As I ran, I felt the tension slipping off me like water. My steps grew lighter, my breathing easier. Dad was pleased with me.

And Jonas would leave Dad alone now. He'd move on to something else.

But I couldn't shake off Brody's words. *Smoothing things over*. I remembered his fury at the Eye fence the day before. And later that night at his house.

It was hard to believe the same guy had showed up tonight at the Eye, beaming with goodwill and inviting me to drop by sometime.

I slowed my steps and grinned. Maybe I wouldn't go to the community center just yet. Maybe I'd head over to the Bilks'. Specifically, to Lauren Bilk.

I'd been thinking about Lauren a lot. Wishing we could have a second meeting. A normal meeting this time, one that didn't involve me with my arm in a planter. Or Brody yelling.

I also wanted to find out what was behind Brody's weird change in mood. Had he been sincere? Lauren might be able to help me figure that out.

So I was going to take Brody up on his invitation. I was going to drop by.

Especially since I knew he wasn't home right now.

Two women stood at the end of the Bilks' drive. They were frowning up at the house.

"It's a disgrace," said one of the women. "Jonas complains about a

Ferris wheel ruining the neighborhood.
Meanwhile, he has someone in there
screaming."

"Last night the screams ruined my
dinner," her friend said.

I paused, listening. So I'd been right!
Somebody at the Bilks' was in trouble.
Brody had lied about the cry for help
coming from the TV.

The first woman sniffed. "If you ask
me, they've got an exotic pet in there.
One they're not supposed to have.
That's what's making those noises.
I'm guessing an orangutan."

The women barely glanced at me as
I passed. "*I* bet it's a wild parrot," said
the second woman.

I sprinted up to the Bilks' front door.
I was about to ring the bell.

A man's loud voice from inside
stopped me.

"You say one word to anyone and
I'll send you packing!"

The next voice was a female one, softer, not yelling. I couldn't hear what she was saying. Whatever it was, she didn't get to say much of it. The man cut in.

"Every family has its secrets. Keep ours quiet, missy. Or I'll throw you out, niece or not!"

That had to be Jonas Bilk. And he was threatening Lauren.

The two women were wrong. The screamer from upstairs wasn't an exotic pet. It was a person. I'd heard her beg for help.

I figured it was someone Jonas had gotten mad at. Had beaten up, maybe. He was like Brody—tall, big-shouldered. Someone smaller wouldn't have a chance against him.

I couldn't let him beat up Lauren. I had to get in there.

Chapter Eight

I wrenched at the doorknob. I'd ram the door open if necessary. Or kick it in. I'd been practicing horizontal dance kicks against the trunk of the maple tree at home.

But the door wasn't locked, and I shoved it too hard. I skidded onto the smooth marble floor and lost my balance. I fell backward, my legs sticking up like antenna.

So much for being a suave rescuer.

The foyer was dim. After the bright sun, I couldn't see right away. "Lauren!" I yelled.

I got up. I saw her—and Jonas.

They were by the painting of the woman holding the white flower. In the shadowy foyer, the flower had a supernatural glow.

They gaped at me. Jonas opened his mouth. I braced myself to be yelled at.

Instead, tightening his face muscles, Jonas got control of himself. It was obviously a huge effort for him. It almost hurt to watch.

"Got stuff to do," he muttered, and he shuffled into the room behind him.

The room was an office. A computer sat on a gleaming mahogany desk. Papers were stacked to one side.

It was a very tidy desk—the desk of a control freak. No wonder Jonas was angry at Lauren. Having someone blab family secrets would be too untidy for him.

Jonas sat down at the desk. He reached for the phone.

In a low voice I told Lauren, "You're not safe here. I have an aunt you can stay with. The nice thing about Aunt Mary's house is that it's scream-free. No one's being tortured."

Lauren broke into a nervous giggle. "You have the wrong idea, Chaz. No one's being tortured. It's just—"

She hesitated. "Uncle Jonas is angry at me because I want to tell the neighbors the truth. They hear the screams. They're upset."

"Okay, so no one is being tortured. Then why the screaming? Does somebody upstairs have a weird medical condition? I've heard of people who can't stop swearing. But *screaming*?"

"Don't be ridiculous, Chaz. It's not a medical condition. I can't say any more than that."

I glanced up at the portrait of the woman with the white flower. The first time I saw the painting, I'd thought how pretty the woman was—like Lauren. Now I noticed the dark trees around her. Dark, like the family secret. They made the painting kind of ominous.

Lauren followed my glance. "That was my great-grandmother. She grew up in this house. It must have been fun for her. Not many people lived around here then. She had the forest pretty much to herself."

In the next room, Jonas barked into the phone, "You got photos. You got your sample. Now let's talk money."

Lauren whispered, "Uncle Jonas isn't as mean as he seems, Chaz. He's just kind of uptight. He's having problems with the *North Van Express*. Like a lot of newspapers these days, it's losing money."

"Yeah, I get that," Jonas was saying impatiently. "But I can't move forward till I have a guarantee from you, Hans. A written one."

As he talked, Jonas flipped a pencil around in his fingers. Then he paused, gripped the pencil hard and snapped it in two.

Kind of uptight. Right.

"Let's get out of here," I said abruptly. "We can grab a soda at the community center. I'll do some dance steps for you."

Away from the house, Lauren grew more relaxed. She teased me about my first appearance at the Bilks'. "Cramming your arm into a pot of soil. What dance move would that be?"

In the dance studio, she sat down on a bench. I dragged a stepladder over.

Then I got some mats from the studio shelves and piled them behind the stepladder.

I got my tap shoes out of my locker. "I'll show you the routine I've been practicing," I told Lauren. "It's very formal. The important thing for me is to stay dignified. Dignity, always dignity."

I did a few whirls around the floor as a warm-up. Then I tap-danced backward onto the first stair of the stepladder. I danced on and off the step several times.

She was smiling. That energized me. That put music into my head. I danced up to the second stair and down again. I repeated that. Then I tap-danced backward up to the third step. I repeated that too.

Then I tap-danced backward up to the fourth step.

Except that there was no fourth step. My feet met air.

Lauren shrieked. She stood up. But there was nothing she could do. It was too late.

I dropped my mouth into a wide, horrified O. I flailed my arms. I fell on the mats. I kicked my legs straight up.

And spun into a backward somersault.

I jumped into standing position on the floor behind the mats and took a deep bow.

It was Lauren's turn to gape. Then, relaxing, she laughed and clapped. "You had the whole thing planned!"

I nodded, pleased. "I based it on a Gene Kelly routine. I even used one of his lines—*Dignity. Always dignity.* Of course, he meant just the opposite. He believed that people should have fun watching dancers. Dance doesn't have to be serious all the time."

"Neither does life. Tell that to my uncle though." Lauren sighed.

I wanted to ask her about that. Then Gene Kelly's voice sang out *"Gotta dance!"*

It was my ringtone. I pulled the phone from my jeans pocket.

Dad said, "Son, I'm at the Eye. Someone just tried to break in. The guard chased him away."

Dad sounded more tired than I'd ever heard him. I didn't get it. We had a guard now. He'd done his job.

"So that's good, isn't it?" I asked.

There was a pause. Dad inhaled loudly. "The intruder used steel cutters to chop two massive holes in the fence. That means a security guard isn't enough. I'm going to have to invest in video surveillance."

I heard something else in his voice, and it scared me. Dad didn't just sound tired. He sounded hopeless. Defeated.

As his next words proved.

"I don't know if I can afford to go on with the Eye, Chaz. Not when someone wants me out of here so bad. It may be too much for me."

Chapter Nine

I told Lauren curtly, "I have to go see Dad. I'll walk you home. Just give me a minute."

I went out to the hall. I dropped coins into a drink machine. I pressed the soda selection button. The soda can started to fall—then stuck.

Like I'd actually expected something to go right.

I slammed the side of the machine. The machine shook, but the soda can stayed put.

Lauren joined me. "I heard some crashing noises," she said.

She pressed hard on the soda selection button. The can clanked to the bottom. She handed it to me.

I popped the tab, let her have the first swig, then downed the rest myself. I told her what had happened.

"Now I want the Eye to stay open," I finished. "Sure, Dad closing it would mean I could go to dance camp. But I don't care. I can't stand how hopeless Dad sounded. That isn't Dad. Not *my* dad."

I crumpled the can in my fist.

Lauren blurted, "I'm so sorry about all that's happened. I hate that Uncle Jonas wrote that stupid story. I'm embarrassed someone in my family would behave like that."

I couldn't trust myself to make any comments about Jonas Bilk. I lobbed the can into the recycle bin.

She said, "Let me come with you to the Eye. You could use a friend right now."

I shrugged. I wasn't feeling all that sociable. I turned and walked out of the community center. She followed.

"It was a guy in a navy hoodie," said the security guard. "Big, tall, broad-shouldered. I reached through the fence. I almost had him."

Two cops had arrived at the Eye. One was taking notes on what the guard said. The other was checking out the two jagged holes in the fence.

Dad stood listening, face ashen, eyes dull.

Lauren murmured to me, "I know you're thinking the fence cutter was Brody.

But it couldn't have been. Brody has his weekly lesson. He never misses it."

"That will be easy for the cops to check on," I said coldly.

She drew back, and I knew I'd hurt her feelings. But I was too upset to care.

I looked up at the Eye. It curved above the trees, bright and beautiful. I thought of all the work Moe, Dad and I had done to scrub off the black paint.

I thought of all the money Dad had put into the Eye. All the dreams.

And how, from the start, people had given him trouble over it. First Jonas, complaining about it in the *North Vancouver Express*. Then the paint vandal. Now a fence cutter.

George Ferris had at least enjoyed success for a while. At the 1893 Chicago World's Fair, his Ferris wheel grew so popular it was known as Queen of the Midway. Inspired, George had an idea to make it more magical at night.

He strung up that new invention, light-bulbs, all around the wheel.

After the world's fair, George had the wheel moved to a different part of Chicago, then to St. Louis. People turned against him. They wouldn't ride it. A wrecking company bought the wheel and dynamited it. The company sold the steel for scrap metal.

George Ferris died poor and alone. He was buried without any kind of marker. Later, Ferris wheels and Eyes caught on big-time. Yet to this day no one knows where the man who invented them is buried.

The thought shoved itself back into my brain. *At least George enjoyed success for a while. That's more than Dad's had.*

Lauren slid her hand into mine. "I'm so sorry, Chaz. I'm keeping the family's secret about the screaming. But I swear, if I thought they were involved in the problems with the Eye, I would tell. You have to believe me."

I looked at her. Her blue eyes were full of sympathy, nothing else. She wasn't hiding anything. I believed her.

I laced my fingers through hers. It was my way of telling her I was glad she'd come along. It wasn't the kind of thing I could say. But I think she knew.

In my dreams, I never had vertigo. I danced off the ground and into the air. I cartwheeled. I spun. I tap-danced on stars.

That night my dream was different. Lauren was calling to me from Earth. I tried jumping down. But the air bounced me back up like an invisible trampoline.

"Chaz!" she shouted. "I told you too much! Uncle Jonas is going to send me away!"

"You didn't tell me anything," I called back.

I jumped again. The air bounced me back. I punched it—*pow-ditty-pow-pow!*—like in my new routine. I kept punching, and slowly I pushed through, down to earth.

Lauren came into view. She was in the woods, by the fence. She wasn't yelling anymore. She was as still as a statue.

"Almost there!" I punched through more air. Then, with a *whish*, the air gave way. I landed in the grass, in the wildflowers.

I scrambled up. "Lauren?"

But it wasn't Lauren now. It was the woman with the glowing white flower.

She held the flower up to me, closer and closer. The flower expanded. The white petals turned into a floodlight and blinded me.

Chapter Ten

When I woke, I sat up and yelled,
"AAAGGGHHH!"

From outside my open window came
a startled exclamation. "*Chaz*?"

It was Dad. He probably thought I
was being murdered. Or that a baboon
was in the house.

I swung out of bed and padded over
to the window.

Below me, outside the front door, stood Dad, with Jonas and Brody Bilk.

Dad gazed up at me in astonishment. Jonas looked impatient. I had interrupted them.

Brody kept his gaze down. He was reading a large slim book.

I called down, "Sorry, Dad. Weird dream."

I headed toward the bathroom. I needed a hot shower to get that dream out of my mind. That weird, glowing white flower.

I stopped. Speaking of weirdness—

What were the Bilks doing at our house?

I went partway downstairs, just enough to hear the conversation through the open front door.

Jonas's voice oozed up to me. It was oily and fake friendly.

"...an admirable effort, Don. Everyone agrees on that. You worked hard. You built your dream—North Vancouver's first Eye. You put us on the map, Don. Up there with London, Shanghai, Rio de Janeiro."

Jonas sounded like he was on Dad's side. I didn't get it.

Jonas's too-smooth words flowed on. "But you've had some problems, Don. Some controversy. And two cases of vandalism."

The newspaper publisher clicked his tongue. "I'm a businessman too, Don. I know how problems take their toll on a person. Heck"—a bark of laughter—"they take their toll on a person's bank account!"

I edged down another couple of stairs. Now I could see Dad and Jonas and Brody, deep in his book. Dad's shoulders were hunched. His head drooped.

Ice climbed my spine. I realized what had happened over the past day or so. Jonas had sucked the life out of Dad.

Jonas said, "I'm going to help you, Don. If you'll let me."

No, I thought. Don't listen to him, Dad. Jonas doesn't want to help you. He has some other reason for being here. Something he isn't telling. That's what Jonas is all about—secrets.

Jonas fished in his shirt pocket. He brought out a rectangular piece of paper.

He said, "This is a check for you, Don. I think you'll find the amount to be more than fair."

Dad didn't take the check. Didn't move. "I don't understand."

"I'm offering to buy you out, Don. Take over the Eye. Relieve you of your problems."

Sweat shone on Jonas's forehead. He badly wanted Dad to accept.

Why? What would a money-losing newspaper publisher want with a money-losing Ferris wheel?

Dad didn't reach for the check. But he didn't take his eyes off it either.

No, Dad, I thought. Don't do it.

With the back of his hand, Jonas wiped the sweat off his forehead. "You can build an Eye somewhere else. Just take this one apart and move the pieces. Look at it that way—you're *making* money."

Dad didn't take the check. He didn't say anything. But he nodded slowly. This made sense. Jonas was getting to him.

How could Jonas afford to buy out Dad? That made no sense.

Jonas talked on, his words washing over Dad. Wearing him down like water wears down a stone—if nothing stops it.

"The Eye is a good idea. This just wasn't the place for it. I'll take the land over. It's the right thing to do."

Give me a break, I thought. You're into doing the right thing like I love heights. There's some other reason you want the property.

Dad reached for the check.

Well, Jonas hadn't sucked the life out of *me*.

"No!" I shouted.

They looked at me. Even Brody glanced up from the slim book he was so focused on.

There were so many things I wanted to say. *Liar, liar, pants on fire* would have been a satisfying start. But it was Dad I had to get through to.

I blurted, "George Ferris did that. He set up his wheel somewhere else."

"Uh…sure," said Jonas, bewildered.

Jonas didn't know what I was talking about. But Dad did. Once George moved his Ferris wheel, it was the end of him.

Dad held my glance for a long moment.

He didn't take the check. He put both hands in his pockets. He said, "Give me a day to think about your offer, Jonas. To talk about it with my son."

Jonas kept smiling, but his eyes flashed with annoyance. He didn't want to wait. He wanted this deal done.

"Of course," he said. "I'll hold the offer open until tomorrow."

He walked down our path to the sidewalk.

Brody followed. But first he shot Dad and me a look. Not a hostile look though. It was kind of a wistful look.

I didn't have time to think about that. In the next twenty-four hours, I had to find out why money-strapped Jonas was so anxious to buy the Eye property from Dad.

And talk Dad out of selling.

Chapter Eleven

Dad replaced the phone. "That was my realtor. She said land values around here haven't shot up. If anything, they've softened."

He shrugged. "So Jonas can't be looking to flip the land and make a profit."

"He wants the land for something," I said.

What, though? I executed three side-steps and a spin. I needed to get my brain cells working on it. *What made this particular property so attractive to Jonas?*

"Not bad, Gene," Dad observed.

"What? Oh—thanks. Sorry. I..." I trailed off, embarrassed. I guessed it didn't look very businesslike, lapsing into Gene Kelly mode.

Dad waved off the apology. "You've been decent about supporting me with my Eye dreams and schemes. The least I can do is support you in your dancing."

I hesitated. I was used to being on the defensive about dancing. To him ranting about what a loser career choice it was.

But he was smiling. "You got a routine down for the contest?"

He hadn't asked me about the contest before.

"Yeah, I think so. Lots of punching and..."

I paused. I was back in my dream. I was punching my way down through the air to reach Lauren. Only it wasn't Lauren when I got there. It was her great-grandmother, with that glowing white flower.

"The contest is Saturday, isn't it?" Dad asked. "I'll be there, watching. If you don't mind," he added.

"No, that'd be great," I said. I smiled back.

I was obsessed with that dream. For some reason I needed to figure out why the dream was staying with me. It was like the dream was trying to show me an idea buried deep in my mind that I couldn't reach.

The next day was gray. It was hot and still. According to weather reports, a storm was brewing.

I took tickets. I helped people on and off the Eye.

The twenty-four-hour mark had come and gone. Dad was on the phone with the bank. He was trying to find a way to stretch his money, to find out if he could get another loan.

I wondered when Jonas Bilk was going to show up.

Moe relieved me for lunch. When I came back, he'd leave. He had the afternoon off. His dad had invited him to watch a surgery from the operating-room gallery.

I went to the office. Dad was still on the phone. He shook his head at me.

Two guys from the fence company arrived. With Dad busy, I offered to show them the section that needed repairing.

I led them through the woods. Again I noticed the quiet. It was like stepping into another world. No wonder Lauren's great-grandmother had hung out in the woods.

When we got within view of the fence, it was back to the real world again.

The two jagged holes stared at me like oversized eyeballs as the men inspected the fence.

The holes reminded me of the short gray-haired man with the gold-rimmed glasses. He had stared at me too. He had told me to *look up, up!* at the birds.

He had claimed to be a bird-watcher. But he couldn't tell a goldfinch from a robin.

I realized I was punching the air, like in my dance routine. The men from the fence company watched me in surprise.

"This is how I think," I explained to them.

They glanced at each other and shrugged, as if to say, *Kids*. They went back to jotting down notes.

I didn't care what they thought. I was remembering something else.

Brody Bilk, showing up at the Eye to make friendly. Brody had wandered into the woods. When I followed, he aimed his camera up into the dark evergreens. What kind of photographer would do that?

No photographer. Just like a person who mistook a robin for a goldfinch was no bird-watcher.

People were awfully anxious for me to think they were looking up.

Maybe it was time I looked down.

I crouched in the grass and the wild-flowers. It took a moment for my eyes to get used to the shade.

White wildflowers were scattered pretty evenly through the grass. I looked closer. Except in one patch, where—

Where grass had been pulled away. Where a hole yawned at me.

Someone had dug one of the flowers up.

Brody? Is that what he'd been doing here? I'd heard something clanking in his knapsack, like spoons.

Or…spades.

I flattened the grass around another flower. I leaned in close. I had barely noticed the wildflowers before. They were just wildflowers.

No. They weren't.

The petals were too big. They curved wide and then met in a point. Two gold stamens with rounded ends hung out. Like two tiny people taking a bow.

I'd lived in this area all my life. I'd played, jogged and skied at Grouse Mountain. But I had never seen this type of flower here till now.

I'd seen it in one other place though—the portrait of Lauren's great-grandmother. The woman had, as a girl in the 1920s, played in these woods. In those days, the woods stretched for miles, unspoiled and undeveloped.

I leaned back on my heels and punched the air a couple of times. I thought about land.

Dad's realtor had said land values were soft. So Jonas, already facing money problems, wouldn't be looking to profit off land.

But what if it wasn't the land he was interested in?

What if it was something that grew on the land?

I felt the first spatter of raindrops as I ran back to the office. I pushed the office door open so hard it crashed against the wall. "Dad?"

No reply. No sign of Dad. His phone lay on the desk. Typical. He'd forgotten it.

I checked his recent calls. The name I didn't want to see popped up first. *Jonas Bilk.*

I played it out in my mind. Jonas called and Dad agreed to sign the deal. He could be on his way to the Bilks'.

I heard the door open again. I whipped around.

I wanted so badly for it to be Dad. But it was Moe.

My buddy stared at the floor. He wanted something but wouldn't ask. Asking was too much bother. Asking involved vocabulary.

Even in my panic, I had to smile. "The surgery," I said. "You have to go."

Moe nodded. I thought of asking him to stay. I didn't though. Watching someone get sliced and diced wasn't my idea of a great afternoon. But it meant a lot to him.

"Go on," I said. "I'll close up. Nobody's going to come in this weather. And I have to find Dad. It's…"

It's life or death, I almost said. But that was too corny. Or was it? The Eye was Dad's dream. And dreams were what you lived for.

Moe left. I locked the office and the front gate.

I ran down the hill. The sky spat out more raindrops, big, heavy ones that hit the pavement like stones.

I had to reach Dad in time.

Chapter Twelve

I rang the Bilks' doorbell once. No answer. I pressed my finger on it. Still nothing. I pounded the door with my fist.

From inside, silence.

Yet a car was parked in the curving driveway.

I tried the door. Locked. I ran around to the back. The stone terrace surrounded a swimming pool. The rain, now turned to hail, hammered the water. Splashes rose like geysers.

I shoved my face against the glass doors.

Jonas was hunched over his desk examining something. He was alone.

I felt a glimmer of relief. Dad wasn't here—yet.

I tried the window handle. It turned. I stepped inside. My soaked runners squelched against the marble floor.

But Jonas didn't hear. He was wearing earbuds.

I tapped his shoulder.

He removed the buds. He turned around with the snarl that was his version of a smile.

"Another of your dramatic entrances! I shouldn't be surprised."

I never got to reply. From upstairs, screams rang out. They went on and on, each one higher and louder than the one before.

Jonas smashed his fist down on his desk. "Enough!"

He stomped out of the room. I heard his feet pounding up the winding marble staircase.

No one's being tortured, Lauren had said. Maybe not, but somebody up there was in trouble. Someone was suffering big-time. And Jonas had not been wearing a love-thy-neighbor expression just now. The screamer's situation was about to get way worse.

I started after Jonas. Dad losing his property was one thing. This could be someone's life.

As I passed the desk, I knocked over a tin wastebasket. The basket went flying.

I straightened it. A crumpled piece of paper had fallen out. I picked it up. I was about to drop it back in.

Then, without meaning to, I read the first few words.

I stopped. Smoothing the paper, I read the rest of it.

I sank into Jonas's chair. I stared at the words for a long moment. Now I understood about the screams. About the cry for help, and Jonas's furious "Enough!"

There was something I should do about the screams. Something I should say.

But it could wait, I decided.

Because my gaze fell to the desk. To what Jonas had been hunched over.

It was photos. Close-up shots of the white flowers in the woods. They were taken from every angle, with shots of stems to leaves to stamens to creamy petals.

But you wouldn't need to be close to get these photos. You could snap them with a zoom lens—like the short gray-haired man had been holding. That's what he'd been up to. Not bird-watching.

I heard shouting upstairs. Jonas could storm back down here at any moment. I had to be fast.

I picked up the letter. It was on gold-edged stationary, with gold lettering at the top: *Hans von Driezel, Collector of Rare Plants*.

The gray-haired man! I was sure of it. I could hear his brisk, accented voice. *See the birds! How they fly about. So graceful.*

It was Hans I'd heard Jonas talking to on the phone. Jonas had snapped, *I can't move forward till I have a guarantee from you, Hans. A written one.*

Upstairs, a cellphone rang. The shouting stopped.

I read on.

Dear Mr. Bilk,

As you requested, I am setting this down in writing. From photographs

I've taken, I am almost sure the flowers in the woods are a rare breed of snow orchid—thought to be extinct.

I need you to bring me a specimen. I will study it under a microscope. If these are, as I suspect, genuine snow orchids, I will buy them from you for—

It was a large number. I had to blink to make sure all the zeroes in it were real. It was way more than Dad had paid for the Eye property.

I let out a whistle. No wonder Jonas, though in financial trouble, wanted to buy the land from Dad. By law, the woods were a protected ecosystem. Dad respected that. But Jonas wouldn't. Once the land was his, he'd let Hans von Driezel dig up the snow orchids. He'd never have to worry about money again.

I folded the letter. I tucked it into my pocket. I kept thinking.

With his newspaper story, Jonas had fired up public anger. On the Eye's opening day, protesters had scared customers off. Later, Jonas sent someone to vandalize the Eye, then to cut holes in the fence.

From the guard's description, the vandal was Brody. It made sense. Brody had dug up the snow orchid. Brody did what his dad ordered. He was Jonas's henchman.

All oily smiles and fake sympathy, Jonas had shown up on our doorstep. He'd offered to buy the property from Dad.

Now I knew why. Now I could stop the deal.

I pushed out the office door and into the marble foyer. I stopped. The house was silent.

I looked around. The only person I saw was the woman in the painting. It seemed she was staring at me over the glowing white flower. Warning me with her bright blue eyes.

I swung around.

Brody was at the top of the stairs. He was holding the slim book. He studied me for a moment, as if I were a specimen like the flower he'd stolen. As if I were something he was trying to understand.

Then he said, "My dad's going to meet your dad at the Eye. Your dad's agreed to sign."

Chapter Thirteen

I pushed out the front door. The hail had turned to rain—thick, silver sheets of it.

The car that had been parked along the Bilks' wide, crescent-shaped driveway was gone. That phone call had been from Dad. While I'd been concentrating on the photos and letter, Jonas had talked with Dad. He'd left the house.

I phoned Dad's cell. *Please be there. Please answer.*

Ringing. Then voice mail kicked in.

I closed my eyes. I lifted my face and let the rain sluice down it. I said, "Dad. Don't sign. Wait for me."

I ran back up the hill to the Eye. It was tough going. The rain was so thick I couldn't see where sidewalk ended and road started.

By the Eye's gate, I thought I saw a figure. "Dad?" I shouted.

The figure drew back, blurred into shadow. Or maybe there hadn't been a figure at all. Maybe it was a trick of the gushing rain and wind.

The gate was open. Maybe Moe had decided to come back and wait out the rain.

Then I noticed the lock on the gate. It had been smashed. Someone had broken in.

I ran to the office. It was empty.

All at once—
Can you believe, baby, how good it feels
Falling in love on a Ferris wheel?
Dad's phone.

The music was coming from the Eye. I ran toward it, thinking Dad was calling his own number because he couldn't remember where he'd left his phone. He was hoping somebody would pick up. This would be my chance to tell him about the snow orchid.

I jumped up onto the platform. The door to the control booth stood open, its glass window smashed. Whoever had broken through the gate had got into the booth too. Some Eye fanatic who just couldn't wait for a ride?

I didn't see anyone. Maybe they'd been and gone.

The phone was on a seat inside the first gondola. I stepped inside. I bent to reach for it.

Then someone was gripping my T-shirt collar, twisting it tight so I couldn't breathe. He placed his other hand on the back of my head. Lightning fast, he pushed me forward. Smashed my forehead into the window.

I slid from the seat to the floor. Black speckled my vision. The speckles were melding together. I was going to pass out.

Something stopped me. A loud noise. The gondola door, slamming shut. I sat up.

I felt the gondola move. It was gliding backward and up.

The Eye was turning.

I tried to pull myself up to the seat. I couldn't. I was weaker than a baby. I couldn't even make my hands into fists.

I felt in my jeans pocket for my phone. It wasn't there. I tried all the pockets. I looked around the gondola for it.

It was gone. The person who tackled me had taken it.

Dad's phone!

I looked around. It, too, was gone.

This person did *not* want me calling for help.

My hands still felt like marshmallows. I pressed my elbows into the seat. I put all of my weight on them. It practically killed me, but I pushed myself up.

I landed sideways on the seat. A dancer? I was more like a beached whale.

I lay there, heaving in big ragged breaths. I was able to think again. Sort of.

Who would do this to me?

Brody. He'd followed me from his house. If the Eye deal went through, it meant a lot of money for his family. He wanted to stop me from warning Dad.

But why take both phones? The Eye would complete its first revolution.

The gondola would swing back down to the platform. I'd get out. I'd get help.

It didn't make sense. Neither, I realized suddenly, did the idea of Brody following me. I'd seen a figure in the rain, but the figure had been ahead of me, not behind.

Then something else bothered me. Big-time.

The Eye stopped moving.

I hadn't looked out the window before. I'd figured a bashed-up forehead was enough without getting dizzy.

Now I struggled to sitting position. I took a deep breath. I looked out.

The Eye had halted at its halfway point. I was at the top.

The rain had eased off. The air was clearing. The clouds were melting into blue sky.

If only I could keep looking at the sky, I'd be fine. But I had to look down.

I had to see what was going on. I pressed my palms against the window. I felt the all-too-familiar stomach lurch. But I forced my gaze to drop.

By the office, Dad was standing beside his car. He had his head down, his hands shoved in his pockets.

Another car pulled up. Jonas Bilk got out.

The deal was going to go through. Trapped up here, I couldn't stop it.

Chapter Fourteen

I opened my mouth to yell. What came out instead was my lunch.

In frustration I pounded the window. That did no good. Dad couldn't hear. The glass was too thick.

He wouldn't have heard even if I'd yelled.

I shut my eyes. It helped that the Eye wasn't moving. My stomach, which had been preparing for another liftoff, had settled. I was able to think.

The glass was too thick. To attract Dad's attention, I'd have to have to open the gondola door.

And then—the earth would spin up at me. I'd lose all sense of balance. I might even fall out of the gondola.

My old enemy, vertigo. It got me every time.

Rage filled me. I hated the hold vertigo had over me. I hated being its victim. Most of all, I hated that it was going to cost Dad the Eye.

I staggered to the door. Closing my eyes, I heaved the door open.

Fresh, cool air rushed in. Gripping the sides of the doorway, I glanced down. Dad and Jonas were walking to the office. Jonas was talking. Gloating, I guessed. Dad still had his head down.

The vertigo started. The Eye grounds,

the trees, surged up at me. They fell back. They surged again.

I tried to shout but, sure enough, I puked. I swayed back inside the gondola. It was useless. I didn't know what to do.

More cool air floated in. The breeze swished around me. I heard a voice whispering, *You don't know what to do. So what do you do?*

I…I dance, I thought. When things are awkward and I don't know what to do, I dance.

But that was on the ground. On solid earth. I couldn't do that here. No way.

Just dance!

I knew there was no voice. It was just the breeze.

Still—

Okay, I thought. I'll try.

I stuffed seat cushions into the bottom half of the doorway. If my feet hit them, I'd know to back up.

Clenching my fists, I stood. I looked straight ahead, into blue sky. I began to punch the air. *Pow! Pow!* I punched harder. There was no dancer-like grace to my punches. They were clumsy. I was using my rage, like I'd done the other night.

But rage was good. Rage took concentration.

Slowly the sickness ebbed away. I was able to think. I had to make Dad hear me. I opened my mouth. Words, not barf, came out. "Dad! Up here!"

I shouted about the snow orchid. About the man with the glasses. About Jonas and his lies.

I got my beat back. I jumped up and down. I sidestepped. I even spun. I, not vertigo, owned the space. I owned *me*.

I roared like a madman. I lost track of what I was saying. All I knew was that I had to make noise.

And then the Eye began to move.

Like a beach ball, the Eye rolled down the sky. It dipped into the dark, green woods. It sloped past the ferns, the wildflowers.

It drew back into the clearing. Sun filled the gondola again. The ground spun up at me. I sank to my knees. I clutched my stomach.

No one was by the office. Were they inside? Was Dad signing the deal?

The Eye slowed. The gondola eased onto the platform. It slid along-side the control booth. It rested.

I saw a pair of feet in patent-leather shoes.

I raised my eyes. Dad was smiling. He held out a hand to me. I took it. He helped me up.

I looked around. The Bilks' car was gone.

Had he signed? I was too scared to ask.

Dad put his arm around my shoulders. "Snow orchid, huh?"

Dad and I were sitting on the edge of the Eye platform. After the storm, the day had become blistering hot. We were working our way through a pitcher of lemonade.

In the woods, a botany prof from the University of British Columbia was examining the snow orchids. People from the city parks department hovered nearby.

A crowd pressed against the Eye fence. Reporters, photographers, TV crews. Curious neighbors. Police stood by to make sure nobody got out of hand.

But it wasn't like that first day. People weren't mad. They were excited. They were quiet—it was like they were all holding their breath. This rare breed of snow orchid was a big deal, a BC legend you could find only in paintings and old photos. So people had thought.

The mayor, who'd jammed out on us that first day, kept phoning Dad. Suddenly he was Dad's best friend. The city would take care of protecting the precious patch of snow orchids, he said. The city would handle twenty-four/seven security for the whole Eye grounds.

Moreover, they would pay Dad to let them set up a nature center at the Eye. People who came to ride the Eye would be able to visit the center. They could view the snow orchids through a telescope.

"Get ready for lots of visitors," the mayor had boomed through the phone. "You have the only Eye in the world sharing space with a rare flower, I'd say. Or rather, *Eye'd* say!" He yelped with laughter.

The gate opened. Our first visitor since the news of the snow orchid had gone public.

Well, not a visitor exactly.

The person who'd waited for me at the Eye. Who'd broken through the gate and into the control booth. Following me into the gondola, he'd bashed my forehead against the window. Then he'd set the Eye to go halfway up.

The person who'd tried to stop me from telling Dad about the snow orchid.

I wanted to punch his face in.

But all those people were watching. I had to stay calm. Play it cool.

I walked up to the smiling gray-haired man with the gold-rimmed glasses. "Why'd you do it, Hans?"

Chapter Fifteen

Hans von Driezel shrugged. One bashed skull, more or less, didn't matter to him, I guessed.

He handed me the canvas bag he was carrying. He murmured, "Inside, you'll find the snow orchid Brody dug up. With all the publicity, I don't dare keep it. But I don't want it to die. Please replant it for me."

"Aren't you skipping a minor detail?" I hissed. "You just—"

Hans waved me off. "You have to understand, Chaz. I am a collector. Rare flowers are my passion. They are my life."

I was still fuming. But I was also fascinated, in a numb kind of way. I listened.

"When you are a collector, the object you long to own is the one just out of reach. For me, it was this breed of snow orchid. *No longer in existence*, all the experts said.

"I visited a Vancouver flower show. Jonas Bilk interviewed me for his newspaper. I told him about the snow orchid. I showed him photos. He did what you call a 'double take.' He brought me to see his grandmother's portrait. There it was, the elusive orchid!

"On a media visit to the Eye, Jonas slipped into the woods. He found the orchids—just where they'd been when his grandmother was a girl! But your father owned the land. And legally, it was protected. To dig the orchids up in secret, Jonas would have to get hold of the land himself.

"So Jonas carried out a little plan. He'd get people to protest the Eye. He'd vandalize it. Force your father to sell."

Hans turned to go. But I was rewinding what he'd said. There was something—someone—missing.

I caught him by the arm. "You said Jonas carried out a little plan. But he didn't do it on his own. He got Brody to help him."

"Oh, *Brody*," Hans scoffed, as if the name wasn't worth the oxygen to say. "Brody dug up the orchid. But that was it. He wouldn't have anything else to do with Jonas's plan. He wasn't comfortable with it. He was too busy with his practicing."

I recalled what the security guard had said. He'd glimpsed someone tall and big-shouldered cutting the fence. I'd assumed it was Brody. *But Jonas was tall and big-shouldered too.*

Besides, Brody had been at a lesson, like Lauren said.

Hans was watching me with a sad little smile. "Ah, Chaz. You are so young. So eager for justice. But I admit nothing. You see, you have no proof."

I spluttered, "Sure I do. I'm going to tell the police that you bashed me on the head."

Hans held up his hands. They were gloved. "What is it you say? 'Look, Ma, no fingerprints.'" He chuckled at his little joke.

He walked away.

I didn't know if he'd get away with it. I hoped not. After all, I had his letter.

But Hans was right about one thing. The snow orchid needed to be replanted, without delay.

I carried the bag into the woods.

Later that week, I gave Lauren a ride in the Eye. I thought it might cheer her up. I thought it might cheer *me* up. The Bilks were sending her home to Maple Ridge.

Having lost their chance at a fortune, the Bilks had put their house up for sale. They were selling off furniture, carpets, art. They were too busy for houseguests.

"At least, that's what they told me," Lauren said glumly, as the Eye lifted into the trees. "I think they're punishing me. They know I like you, and you're the person who spoiled things for them. Not that I blame you," she added quickly. "You did the right thing."

"I like you too," I told her. "A lot. And Maple Ridge isn't that far away. Not for a hoofer with a transit pass."

She smiled. I smiled too. I wasn't dizzy. I was vertigo-free.

The Eye rolled higher. I pointed out Lions Gate Bridge, curving over Burrard Inlet like a shiny bracelet. I pointed out the misty ridge on the horizon that just might be Vancouver Island. And, city side, the giant steel golf ball that was the science center.

The Eye sailed by the sun. For an instant the gondola was filled with gold.

Out of barf mode, I finally got it. I understood Dad's dream.

We floated down, into the bright blue, back into the trees.

When the gondola reached the platform, I took Lauren's hand. We stepped out together.

She said, "Thank you, Chaz. Wow! One thing I don't understand though…"

I waited.

"The whole time we were in the Eye, you kept dancing!"

The talent-show coordinator gave me a puzzled look over the top of her glasses. "You're not set to go on for another two hours."

"I'm here to wish somebody luck."

The woman went back to comforting a ballerina. The kid would be performing for the judges in a short while. If she could stop bawling from stage fright.

From the men's washroom, I heard retching sounds. I guessed it was another contestant with a case of the nerves. No surprise. The talent show was high-stress.

I did a few moonwalk steps to try to cheer the ballerina up. She only wept harder.

I went down the hall and through the stage door.

The next performer, a singer, was waiting in the wings. Judges sat at a table in front of the stage. Once they gave the guy the high sign, he'd go on.

I tapped the singer on the shoulder. "Hey, Brody."

Jonas's son jumped. "What *is* it with you and surprise entrances? You trying to freak me out?"

"Nope. To wish you luck. That's one powerful voice you have."

Brody glanced at the judges. They were still conferring over their notes.

A pianist waited onstage, ready to accompany Brody. The slim book was propped on the piano. Brody's music book.

Brody whispered angrily, "Did Lauren tell you? She promised she'd—"

"*You* told me," I interrupted. "With your screams that carried through the neighborhood. That made me think someone was in trouble. You were doing voice exercises."

Brody stared at me. Some of the anger left his face. "My dad hates that I take voice lessons. Me, the jock. The star football player. Mom hates it too."

I grinned. I remembered the woman's voice, begging Brody to stop with the screams. Mrs. Bilk must have misplaced her earbuds that day.

Brody sighed. "You don't know how lucky you are. Your dad's okay with your dancing. I gotta tell you, I've envied that."

I nodded. It made sense now, Brody's hostility. The wistful look he'd shot Dad and me. The clumsy joke he'd made to cover up his singing lessons.

His parents had made him feel singing was something to be ashamed of.

Brody brightened. "So, uh, you really think my voice is powerful?"

"Megawatt."

"Brody Bilk?" called one of the judges.

I held out my hand. "Good luck."

Brody shook it but said, "I was pretty rotten to you. Why are you telling me this?"

I wasn't sure. Maybe because I was impressed that he kept singing even though his parents dumped all over it. Or because he was stuck with a rotten dad and I had a decent one.

Or because I'd suspected him of vandalism.

I couldn't say this. All I could think of was a wisecrack. A lame one at that.

Lame but true. So I said it:

"Because there's more to you than meets the eye."

Melanie Jackson is the author of numerous mysteries for youth, including *The Big Dip* and *Fast Slide* in the Orca Currents series, as well as the popular Dinah Galloway Mystery series. Melanie lives in Vancouver, British Columbia.

orca *currents*

9781554693429 $9.95 PB
9781554693436 $16.95 LIB

Clay Gibson is sure his summer working at the water park is going to be duller than dull. It gets interesting, however, when he learns that someone has been wandering the park in a lynx costume, scaring the staff. When forty thousand dollars is stolen from the till, and his friend is a suspect, boring starts to look good. Can Clay solve the mystery and still keep his head above water?

orca *currents*

9781554691784 9.95 PB
9781554691791 16.95 LIB

Joe "Mojo" Lumby is a champion
on the track. But when he gets caught up in
the mystery of the Margaret rose, he runs into
trouble. Someone thinks Joe knows where a
mysterious treasure is hidden, and will stop at
nothing to get it. In his search for the Margaret
rose, Joe finds himself in a race against his
toughest opponent yet—time.

Titles in the Series

orca currents

orca currents

For more information on all the books
in the Orca Currents series, please visit
www.orcabook.com.